R is for Rocket

Aa Bb Cc Dd Ee Ff

Gg Hh Ii Jj Kk

Ll Mm Nn Oo Pp

Qq Rr Ss Tt Uu

Vv Ww Xx Yy Zz

an ABC book by Tad Hills

schwartz & wade books · new york

Rocket and his friends have fun learning the alphabet.

Rocket finds **a**corns.

Owl draws **a**n **a**ngry **a**lligator.

Bella balances on a ball while
a big blue butterfly watches.

Owl offers a **c**ookie
and a **c**rayon to a **c**row.

"Now will you stop
cawing?" she asks.

Emma **d**igs a **d**eep hole in the **d**irt near the **d**aisies.

In the **e**vening, **E**mma finds an **e**gg.

Fred frolics with fireflies in the field.

Nobody sees **G**oose in the tall **g**reen **g**rass.

Rocket finds a **h**at on a **h**ill and puts it on **h**is **h**ead.

It makes **h**im **h**appy.

Bella plays
in the **i**vy.

It's not a good **i**dea.
It makes her **i**tch.

Owl jumps for joy.

She loves
to fly **k**ites.

A **l**adybug **l**ands on a **l**eaf and **l**istens
to Rocket read a **l**etter from **L**arry.

A **m**ouse on a **m**ushroom shares his **m**ilk.

The waves are **n**oisy.
They make Owl **n**ervous.

Owl is afraid of the **o**cean.

Rocket **p**aints a **p**icture of a **p**eacock. Owl **p**refers her **p**umpkin.

It is **q**uiet, and Owl is
cozy under her **q**uilt.
She falls asleep **q**uickly.

Rocket **r**ests by the **r**iver in the **r**ain.

Bella sits on a stump.

"I'm glad I have this sock," she says.

Rocket's teacher sees two tiny turtles.
"Are you twins?" she asks.

Unfortunately, Mr. Barker can't
fit **u**nder the **u**mbrella.

Bella climbs a **vine** to get a better **view**.

Rocket wonders,
"Is it windy up there?"

Bella plays the **x**ylophone.

"You are a wonder," the Little Yellow Bird yells from across the yard. "You play with zest and zeal."

Ah, the wondrous, mighty, gorgeous alphabet.

For Anne, Bill, and Cathy

Copyright © 2015 by Tad Hills

All rights reserved. Published in the United States by

Schwartz & Wade Books,

an imprint of Random House Children's Books,

a division of Penguin Random House LLC, New York.

Schwartz & Wade Books and the colophon

are trademarks of Penguin Random House LLC.

Visit us on the Web! randomhousekids.com

Educators and librarians, for a variety of teaching tools,

visit us at RHTeachersLibrarians.com

Library of Congress Cataloging-in-Publication Data

Hills, Tad.

R is for rocket : an ABC book / Tad Hills.

—First edition. pages cm

Summary: Rocket the dog, Bella the squirrel, Owl, and

other friends discover the alphabet, from acorns and an

angry alligator to a zig zag drawn by the Little Yellow Bird.

ISBN 978-0-553-52228-0 (hc)

ISBN 978-0-553-52229-7 (glb)

ISBN 978-0-553-52230-3 (ebook)

[1. Dogs—Fiction. 2. Animals—Fiction. 3. Alphabet.]

I. Title.

PZ7.H563737 Raaf 2015

[E]—dc23

2014045439

The text of this book is set in Filosofia.

The illustrations were rendered in oil paint,

acrylic, and colored pencil.

MANUFACTURED IN CHINA

10 9 8 7 6 5 4 3 2 1

First Edition

Random House Children's Books